BRIGID LUCY

and the Princess Tower

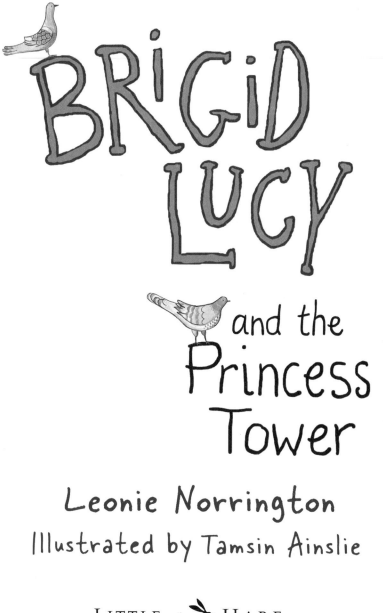

BRiGiD LUCY

and the Princess Tower

Leonie Norrington

Illustrated by Tamsin Ainslie

LITTLE HARE

www.littleharebooks.com

Little Hare Books
an imprint of
Hardie Grant Egmont
Ground Floor, Building 1, 658 Church Street
Richmond, Victoria 3121, Australia

www.littleharebooks.com

Text copyright © Leonie Norrington 2011

Illustrations copyright © Tamsin Ainslie 2011

First published 2011
Reprinted 2011

National Library of Australia
Cataloguing-in-Publication entry

Norrington, Leonie.
Brigid Lucy and the princess tower / by Leonie Norrington ;
illustrated by Tamsin Ainslie.
1st ed.
978 1 921541 70 4 (pbk.)
Norrington, Leonie. Brigid Lucy ; 2.
Princess—Juvenile fiction.
Animals, Mythical—Juvenile fiction.
Ainslie, Tamsin, 1974-
A823.3

Cover design by Vida & Luke Kelly
Set in 13/19 pt Stone Informal by Clinton Ellicott
Printed by WKT Company Limited
Printed in Shenzhen, Guangdong Province, China, October 2011

6 5 4 3 2

This product conforms to CPSIA 2008

Contents

To Ellen Sarah, who often accidentally gets into trouble—LN

For my sister, Jocelyn—TA

Prologue

Hello. Are you a reader person? Yes! I've been waiting for you for ages! Because guess what? I'm a storyteller. I tell all the stories about me and my **best friend**, Biddy. Well, Biddy doesn't know I'm her best friend because she can't see me. I'm invisible.

Don't you adore the word *invisible*? It's just like 'inside visible'. Like, say, for example, if you have underpants underneath your dress. Then the underpants are **invisible**—you can't see them. But they're still there, aren't they? Well, it's the same with me. Although Biddy can't see me and I can't see myself, I'm still here.

What do I look like?

Well, I think I look like this . . .

Or this . . .

But not this . . .

And I definitely haven't got pointy ears or long feet.

How did I meet Biddy?

Me and Biddy came from the country. She used to live on a farm and I used to live in the **Great Bushland**, way past the bottom of her garden.

One day, I was tobogganing down the trunk of a white gum tree. Again. For the one hundredth, millionth time. Boring, boring, boring. When, suddenly, I heard a strange noise. I spun around and slipped.

Zuuup! I flew through the air.

And, **plonk!** I landed in a tangle of hair. This hair was long and soft and attached to a little human girl.

The little girl was sitting under a tree with two huge drippy-tongue dogs. She was crying and cuddling the dogs.

'I'm not going away,' the girl was saying, through sobs and hiccups.

'Going away?' I asked, running onto the top of her head, and out to the end of her nose. 'Where? Can I come? Please, please, please. I've lived in this Great Bushland for one million, six hundred and forty-two thousand years, nearly. I would love to go somewhere else.'

But the little girl just ignored me.

That was when I realised that she couldn't see me, or hear me. So I just ran back up into her hair, and came with her to the city, all by myself.

And it has been so **exciting**! In the city there are millions of people running and rushing and bumping. They say things like, 'Sorry, excuse me. Sorry, pardon.'

And there are lots of magical creatures. One time, in the Centre of Town, we saw a magic pirate man who swallowed a great long deadly sharp silver sword.

And, another time, we saw a silver angel standing as still as a statue. Until she heard coins fall onto her money plate. Then she came to life and sprinkled stardust on Biddy's shoulder, and some fell on me. It was **splendiferous**.

But the bestest thing of all about being with Biddy is that, each night, Biddy's mum reads us stories from books. The stories are about all the magical creatures that I'd never heard of before I met Biddy. They are called elves and witches and pillywiggans.

The Great Bushland where I'm from is full of magical creatures, such as tiny flying ympes, and beautiful nefariouses, and foul-breathed fillikizard dragons. They act the same as the fairies and witches and dragons in Biddy's storybooks. But they look totally different.

Here, let me draw you
a picture . . .

ympes

fillikizard
dragon

nefarious

Don't I miss the Great Bushland?

No way! I love the city to infinity.
And I totally **adore** living with Biddy.
Although sometimes it is a bit annoying
that she can't see me, or hear what
I say. Or when she does boring stuff
like watching TV, or playing computer
games, or listening to her music on her
headphones.

But Biddy only does those things
because she thinks that the city is too
totally **boring**. She says there is nothing
exciting to do. This is because Mum says
we are not allowed to go anywhere by
ourselves, in case we get kidnapped by
the big-bad-stranger-persons or we get
run-over-and-squashed-down-flat-by-a-car.

But I think we can do exciting things anywhere.

So, that's the problem. (You know how all stories have to have a problem? Well that is the problem for this story.) Biddy thinks her life in the city is boring and I love it. Shall I tell that story?

Okay. Wait a minute—I have to start it properly . . .

'Long, long ago . . .'

No, I can't say that because it is happening right now . . .

'Once upon a time . . .'

'Jamie!' Biddy yells.

And suddenly, her head jerks backwards and forwards, sending me flying.

I'm slipping! I grab a strand of hair and cling on. **Bounce! Bounce!**

What is Biddy doing?

She's climbing over the fence. She's going next door to visit Jamie without asking! **Ooh-ah!**

Chapter one
let's pretend

'Jamie, come and **play**,' Biddy yells at Jamie's bedroom door.

(Jamie is a boy. Which is okay. Sometimes you have to have boys in adventures. Especially if there are no girls living in your whole entire street.)

'No,' says Jamie. 'I don't want to.'

'Jamie. Quick, I don't have much time,' Biddy tries to explain, pushing his door open. 'I need someone to play with me. There is no one else.'

But Jamie doesn't listen, so Biddy has to pull him out of his room.

This makes Jamie **yell**, 'Leave me alone! I want to play on my computer!'

'Don't be boring,' Biddy tells him. Then she drags him down the hall and out of the back door into the garden. 'We're going to play princes and princesses and **wicked witches**,' she says.

'I don't like pretending,' Jamie says.

'Imagination is not pretending, Jamie,' Biddy explains. 'It is stories and adventure.' She is using her mummy-being-patient kind-of voice.

'Now,' she says, 'I'm Princess Rapunzel and you're my dog.'

'But I don't want to be a dog,' Jamie frowns. 'If I have to play, I want to be the prince.'

'Don't be silly,' Biddy says. 'We can't have a prince yet. We have to *find* the prince. That's the whole point of the story.'

'I don't want to be a dog,' Jamie says again.

'Not even a big black hunting dog?' Biddy says. She puts her hands on her hips. 'What about a **big scary dog** with gold studs in his collar and four gold earrings like a pirate?' she asks.

Jamie thinks a bit, but then he still shakes his head.

I run up on top of Biddy's head to get a closer look at Jamie. He looks very determined not to be a dog.

Man! What is it with boys? I think. *Why won't they play properly?*

'Come on, Jamie,' Biddy says. She is being as patient as the scoriaks that live in the Great Bushland. Scoriaks are great, **heavy** creatures that live inside rocks and are as patient as the earth growing.

'You can turn into the prince later,' Biddy says. 'And we'll fall in love and get married. Okay?'

'But I don't want to get **married**,' Jamie says.

Which is just too totally silly. Everyone in stories wants to get married and live happily ever after.

So Biddy just ignores that and keeps going with the game.

'Now, if I'm going to fall in love with you, you have to do what you are **told**,' she says.

She stands up, tall and elegant, like a princess. Then she looks down her nose at Jamie and commands, 'Sit!'

Jamie shakes his head again.

But I reckon he is about to change his mind, so I lean out from Biddy's hair, holding onto a strand of her fringe.

'Keep going, Biddy! He'll do it!' I say.

Even though Biddy can't hear me, I can't help but talk to her. And sometimes she does listen, kind of.

'I said, "**Sit!**", pirate dog,' Biddy yells.

Then, just when Jamie is about to sit, someone opens the garden gate, and says, 'Brigid Lucy!' in a very annoyed voice.

It's Biddy's mum! **Oh-oh!** Mum is going to yell at Biddy for coming over to Jamie's place. I quickly run up Biddy's fringe and into her hair to hide. I close my eyes and cover my ears.

'Brigid Lucy, what do you think you are doing?' Biddy's mum yells. She rush-walks across Jamie's garden to where we are playing. Baby Ellen is on her hip, and Biddy's little sister, Matilda, is being towed along behind.

'I've told you not to go **anywhere** without asking me first,' Mum continues.

'I did ask you,' Biddy says, putting on her most innocent face.

'You did not,' says Mum.

'I did so,' Biddy says. 'You just didn't listen to me, because you were talking on the phone.'

Then Mum's face goes all red, and she yells even louder, 'Brigid, go home right now.' As if it is all Biddy's fault that she's in trouble. But it isn't.

Mum **was** talking on the phone when me and Biddy wanted to go to Jamie's. So even if we did want to ask, we couldn't. Because Mum told Biddy she's-not-allowed-to-make-any-noise-while-Mum-is-on-the-phone. So it is Mum's fault, too.

But Mum doesn't admit it is her fault, too. While me and Biddy are walking to the garden gate, we hear Mum tell Jamie in her most polite voice, 'I'm very sorry, Jamie, but Biddy has been a naughty, **naughty** girl. She is not allowed to play any longer.'

Which is not fair. How come she is so nice to him when he was playing, too?

Chapter two
being very good

When we get back home, Mum tells Biddy, 'You are the **naughtiest**-little-girl-in-the-whole-wide-world!'

And, 'What-if-you-had-been-stolen-by-a-big-bad-stranger-person-who-cut-you-into-tiny-pieces-and-sent-you-home-in-an-envelope?'

And, 'How-would-you-like-it-if-I-ran-away-and-you-couldn't-find-me-and-you-were-worrying-yourself-sick?'

Biddy wants to say she's very-very-very-sorry.

But Mum hardly stops yelling before she says, '**Hurry-hurry-hurry**. We have to go to the Centre of Town.'

The Centre of Town!

Yes! That's where the museum is with all the dead-people mummies, and the stuffed magical creatures like the extinct Tasmanian tiger.

I hope we are going to the museum, I think.

But then Mum says, 'I have a very-important-appointment. So I'm going to take you and your sisters to Granny's house.'

'**Hooray!**' I yell. This is the best news of all. Granny lives in the Centre of Town, and she is going to look after me and Biddy, and Miss Getting-All-The-Attention Matilda, and dribbly little Crybaby Ellen, while Mum goes to the very-important-appointment.

Now, the thing is, there is a new rule in Biddy's house since we moved to the city. The rule says: *Naughty-girls-are-not-allowed-to-go-on-outings.* If Mum remembers that Biddy has just been naughty, she won't let Biddy come on the trip to Granny's.

Instead, Biddy will have to stay with Miss Grimes from over the road. Miss Grimes cuts caterpillars and grasshoppers in half with scissors. And she drowns snails and slugs in jars of beer in her vegetable garden. **Yukki-poo-la-drop-kick!**

Biddy really wants to go to Granny's.

Granny is Biddy's absolute favourite grandma. She knows everything about plants and herbs. She knows about magic creatures like fairies and goblins. She even knows about those cheeky yebil yebils that come from the Great Bushland. You know, the ones that look like a slip of a shadow and always trip you up when you are running.

And she knows about bugs (particularly spiders). And she knows all about frogs and snakes and **unicorns**. She is the bestest grandma in the whole entire universe.

Mum tells Biddy to promise that she will be 'the-best-good-girl-that-she-can-possibly-be-for-the-rest-of-the-day'.

Biddy promises she will be good, even though she knows she might not be able to keep the promise. Because how can a person know what's going to happen when it hasn't happened yet?

In the end, the promise did get **broken**, but Biddy wasn't to know that, was she?

She starts by being very good.

Mum says, 'We're going to catch the train, so dress yourself appropriately.'

(*Appropriate* is a schoolteacher word meaning 'okay' or 'right' or 'good'.)

So Biddy doesn't wear her favourite pink plastic high-heeled shoes that make the best clicking noises on the footpath. Mum once said they would get caught in the train door. She said that Biddy would fall-down-through-the-gap-onto-the-train-tracks-and-get-chopped-in-half-by-the-train.

Biddy puts on her second-favourite shoes instead. And she doesn't cry or **scream** when Mum brushes all the tangles out of her fringe, even though it hurts a lot!

But do you think Mum notices how good Biddy is being? No, of course not. Mum is **too busy**, like she always is, trying to feed Crybaby Ellen. And packing the pram. And changing Matilda's shoes onto the right feet, while Matilda screams, 'I do it! I do it!'

Even though she can't, because she is still just a little Getting-All-The-Attention baby-pants.

Chapter three
a train ride

Biddy loves the **clickity-clack, clickity-clack** noise that the train makes as it rocks along the tracks. I do, too. What I like best is when Mum can find four seats that face each other. And then me and Biddy and Matilda all sit together on one side, and Mum and baby Ellen sit on the other one, facing us.

Then Biddy and Matilda bump against each other, and we all sing, '*Clickity, pickity, mickity, quack—the train goes down the railway track. Clackity, clockity, cluckity, click—we bump and sway and don't get sick.*'

Then we go, '**Blaah!**' and pretend to be sick, and Mum tells Biddy and Matilda, 'Girls. Behave.'

But today we can't sing the train song because there are too many people in our carriage. We can't find four spare seats together. So, Matilda has to sit next to Mum and baby Ellen. And me and Biddy have to sit opposite them, next to an evil **witch**. This witch is not a good witch like Granny, the sort that knows all kinds of potions and spells. This witch is a real-proper-evil witch.

It's true! I know it is hard for you human reader people to believe in witches. But we invisible creatures know all about that kind of stuff. I can recognise magical beings anywhere.

Like, we have a nefarious that lives in our Great Bushland. I know all about her. She is beautiful, but totally ancient and grumpy. If ever you went near her, she would gobble you up **dead**.

And I've read heaps about other sorts of witches in Biddy's books.

Some look just like beautiful young women with long white-tipped fingernails.

They always wear shoes with high heels. And they always have beautiful handbags to carry their evilness in.

(You see, if they just had plain, boring handbags, the evilness would **glow** through and everyone would see it.)

I know you are thinking that lots of women are young and beautiful and have pretty fingernails and clothes and shoes and handbags. That's why I am going to tell you a secret. You can use it to check if someone is an evil witch. The secret is: all evil witches are terrified of being touched by children.

By the time human children are Biddy's age, they know when a grown-up person doesn't like kids. And they just don't go near that person. So, when Biddy sees the **evil witch** on the train, she climbs onto the seat next to her, like Mum tells her to. But then Biddy puts her backpack between herself and the witch, and starts looking out of the window.

Mum lifts Matilda up onto the seat next to her, to keep Matilda safe.

Then Mum turns away from Matilda to get baby Ellen out of the pram. Just then, Matilda notices the beautiful woman sitting opposite her with a handbag all covered in bright red sequins and jewels. And Matilda is too little to know about witches, so she makes a big mistake.

She jumps off her seat, reaches out to touch the bag, and says, 'Huddo, I'm Tilly. Dat's **piddy**.'

The witch snatches her handbag away from Matilda's grasp, and glares at Mum. Her lip is curled up. 'Kindly keep your grubby child away from me,' she says.

Mum pulls Matilda back up onto the seat beside her.

Matilda kicks and screams, 'Want the piddy. Want to sit with Bibby.'

(Which is a big fat **fib** because, really, she only wants to sit next to Biddy so she can touch the witch's handbag.)

'Shhh!' Mum says. She gives Matilda Ellen's rattle to play with.

Matilda stops crying and hits the window with the rattle. **Bang! Bang!**

'No, Matilda, darling. Just shake it nicely,' Mum says.

The witch snorts and tuts and rolls her eyes. Then she reaches into her handbag and pulls out her mobile phone, which has just started to ring.

'Hello,' she yells into the phone. 'Yes! Sorry, I can't hear you. There's a child here making an **awful racket**. I'll have to ring you back.'

While all this is going on, I'm sitting up on top of Biddy's head cracking up laughing because I know what Biddy's thinking. Me and Biddy totally dislike people who are rude and **nasty**. We always work out ways to get them back.

So I smile and wait.

And wait.

And wait. But Biddy doesn't do anything.

I crawl down her fringe and look into her eyes. She's just staring out the window, 'being-good'.

'Biddy!' I yell, pointing to the witch. 'This witch is being mean!'

Biddy's eyes slide up to look at the witch from under her eyelashes. I can see she is thinking of ideas. Yes! But then she just shakes her head, puts her thumb in her mouth and looks out the window again.

I **hate** it when Biddy does that! Mum does, too, because she thinks Biddy is 'too-old-to-suck-her-thumb'. But I hate it because Biddy goes into her own little thumb-sucking world. And then she **never** does imagining, and never ever has any exciting ideas.

'Biddy!' I yell. 'I know you promised to be good, but this is ridiculous!'

But she can't hear me, so she just ignores me.

'Well, fine, then,' I say. 'If you are going to be good, I'll just have to get back at the witch all by myself.'

Chapter four

taking revenge

But what can I do to get back at the witch? **Mmmm!** I'll have to have a closer look.

I slip off Biddy's shoulder, and tiptoe down her arm to the edge of her sleeve. The witch's sparkly red handbag is on the seat next to Biddy's backpack. And what's that? There is a piece of thread dangling down from under one of the red sequins. I bet that string ties all the jewels onto the bag.

I wonder what would happen if someone pulled on that string? Would it unravel, so all the jewels and sequins **fell** off? Then, the witch's handbag would be plain and boring.

Everyone would be able to see the evilness inside it. And then they would know that lady is an evil witch. **Yes!** That would definitely get her back for being mean to children.

All I have to do is tie the string from the witch's bag to one of the straps on Biddy's backpack. Okay. I creep further down Biddy's arm, past her elbow, onto her wrist. Now all I have to do is jump onto Biddy's backpack . . .

I lift my arms and bend my knees.

I say, 'Ready? Get settie. **Go!**'

But I can't jump.

It's not that I'm a sooky scaredy-cat chicken-heart or anything. I just don't like leaving Biddy when we are away from her house. Because, what if we get separated? What if she gets lost and I can't find her?

I don't want to be an all-alone, no-best-friend person. What if I never saw Biddy again in my whole entire life? That would be a disastrous catastrophe.

So, instead of jumping, I yell, 'Biddy, you have got to help me.'

But Biddy **ignores** me and keeps sucking her thumb.

Now the train is slowing down. The witch is looking around, ready to get off at the next stop.

'Biddy, look!' I yell again. 'If you don't help me, that witch is going to get away with being mean to your little sister and every other kid in the whole wide world!'

At that moment, Mum notices that Biddy is sucking her thumb.

'Brigid,' Mum says in her soft-but-angry voice. She motions for Biddy to take her thumb out of her mouth.

Biddy doesn't want to stop sucking her thumb. She takes it out of her mouth for just a moment. Then she turns around and **cuddles up** against the back of the seat, so Mum can't see her face any more. Then she puts her thumb back into her mouth.

But, as she looks down at the seat, she notices the loose thread on the witch's handbag.

And she reaches down, picks it up and starts playing with it.

'Yes! Thank you, Biddy,' I yell, running across her wrist and onto her hand. I grab one end of the loose thread and hold onto it, waiting, ready.

Then, the minute Biddy stops playing with it and drops the thread, I run to tie it to a strap on her backpack.

Then, quick as a sunbeam, I run up Biddy's arm, and burrow safely into her hair, to watch what happens next.

The witch stands up, pursing her lips. Her eyes narrow as they glide over Biddy and Matilda and baby Ellen. Then she picks up her handbag and swings it over her shoulder. The string stretches between the backpack strap and the witch's handbag.

Zippp! The string unravels.

The witch walks away.

Tinkle, tinkle, tinkle! The red jewels and sequins rattle to the floor.

The train stops. The carriage doors open. The witch steps out.

I scramble up to the top of Biddy's head to look out of the train window. I can see the witch! All the jewels on her bag are gone. The evilness is showing through.

I'm jumping up and down. 'Look, Biddy! Look!' I yell, pulling Biddy's fringe to make her turn her head around and look out the window. 'We did it!'

But Biddy doesn't turn around, and now the train is moving again.

'No!' I yell. 'Please **wait** a bit longer, train!'

But it doesn't, and I don't see any more.

Now the witch is gone, Mum lets Matilda climb down from her seat.

'Piddy,' Matilda squeals, seeing the jewels sparkling on the carriage floor.

'Look, Mummy. Piddy,' she says, and flops down on the floor to pick them up.

Mum smiles and looks down, but when she sees the jewels, her eyes go all big and guilty. 'Oh, Tilly, don't touch,' she says, jumping up quickly to stop Matilda playing with the jewels.

I can tell Mum knows straightaway that the jewels came from the witch's bag. She looks around in case the witch is still there, ready to **pounce** on Matilda. But the witch is gone.

Then Mum sees the fine string stretched between the jewels to Biddy's backpack. 'Brigid Lucy?' she says.

'Yes, Mum?' Biddy says quickly, taking her thumb out of her mouth and looking around.

'Did you——?' Mum begins.

But then baby Ellen starts crying, so Mum has to pick her up and put her over her shoulder. And then Mum's mouth is so busy going, **'Shhh!'** that she forgets all about the string on Biddy's backpack.

She even lets Matilda collect a whole pile of beads and sequins from the floor.

So me and Matilda and Biddy play and play and play with the jewels. We make piles, and lines, and all sorts of wonderful patterns on the seat.

It is too much f**un**!

Chapter five

the princess tower

Biddy gets bored of playing with the glittery jewels after a while. She goes back to looking out of the window. I do, too, because playing with beads is really a little kid's game. We watch the backs of millions of houses flicking past, with their brightly coloured walls, and their gardens, with plants and spiky weeds and flowers.

Then . . .

Wizz-bang-le-flab!

There is a tower! An ancient stone tower, as tall as tall can be! It reaches up into the clouds, and it's all covered with ancient green moss. Right at the tip of the tower, sitting on top of the rippling orange stone, is a cross.

'**Wow!**' Biddy says. 'That's a Princess Tower.'

And she's right. Of course the tower is a Princess Tower. What else could it be?

'Mum! That's where **Rapunzel** lives,' Biddy says, jumping on the seat. 'That's where Rapunzel hangs down her hair,' she continues, pointing to a tall slit-of-a-window that is cut into the sides of the Princess Tower.

Mum says, 'Will-you-sit-down-Brigid.' And, 'Don't-put-your-shoes-on-the-seat.'

'But, Mum, look!' Biddy says. 'It's a real-life Princess Tower.'

'Brigid Lucy!' Mum says in a do-be-quiet whisper. 'It's not a Princess Tower. It's a cathedral, where people go to pray and talk to God.'

Which is the silliest thing we have ever heard. **Of course** it is a Princess Tower. That shows grown-ups don't know everything. But it is no use trying to convince them, especially when you are trying to be good.

So me and Biddy watch the Princess Tower getting closer and **closer** and bigger and **bigger**. Until it is so close, we have to press our faces against the coolness of the window to see the pointy tip of the cross.

But then we have to stop looking, because Mum is calling us.

Mum packs Ellen into the pram, and tells Matilda to 'hold-on-tight'. Then she tells Biddy to 'concentrate', and 'no-daydreaming', and to 'stay-close-all-the-time'.

We're getting off the train.

Biddy does try to concentrate, she really does. She walks right beside Mum all the way through the station and out onto the street. She 'hangs-on-tight-to-the-pram'. She doesn't suck her thumb or daydream. She can't! Mum is carrying Matilda and walking **very** fast. Her high heels sing, '*Hur-ry, quick-ly, do-not-stop*'. Biddy has to run to keep up.

But then, right in front of us, the traffic lights flash red, and call out, 'Tick! Tick! Tick!' Which means, in robot language, 'Stop! Be safe! Do not cross!'

This is the first time me and Biddy have had a chance to look for the Princess Tower since we got off the train.

There it is! Right there, on the other side of the road. Not the way Mum is heading. The other way. Across the road.

I so wish we could go that way!

'Mum, look!' Biddy says. 'There's the Princess Tower.'

But Mum can't hear her. She is too busy looking at her watch. 'Come on, quickly,' she tells the traffic-light robot. 'We're late. We're in a hurry.' She is being very impatient.

Me and Biddy don't care that the lights are taking simply ages. We love looking at the Princess Tower. It's got all these white curves around the doors, and wonderful coloured glass sparkling in the windows.

But then a **horrible** grown-up person goes and stands right in front of us. We can't see! So Biddy leans right over sideways, trying to look around him. But then another grown-up person just comes and blocks our way. And then so does another, until there are heaps of people crowded all around us. We can't see anything! We are going to miss out on looking at the Princess Tower altogether if we don't get in front of them.

So Biddy lets go of Ellen's pram, just for a second. And then she slips between the people, to the edge of the road, where we can see clearly again.

The Princess Tower is standing tall and magnificent, rising up out of the street, right up to the sky. It has great wooden doors and there is a sign out the front that says 'W-E-L-C-O-M-E'.

WELCOME! We've got to go in! We'll probably never, ever, ever get another chance.

Biddy wants to go in, too, and she does try to tell Mum. 'Mum,' she calls behind her, 'we can go in! It says "Welcome". We're allowed.'

But, at that exact moment, the robot lights go green and say, 'Tick-tick-tick-tick,' very fast. They are telling everyone to, 'Walk quickly! Walk quickly!'

And all the people behind Biddy surge forwards. They take us with them across the stripy lines, and we leave Matilda and Ellen and Mum behind.

Chapter six

the great hall

I don't tell Biddy to run away to the Princess Tower. I really don't. And she doesn't tell herself, either. Both of us know we should stop, and yell out to Mum. To tell her there has been a mistake. That she should come and get us.

But we know Mum will be **angry**. And we don't want to make her even later for her very-important-appointment. And neither of us has ever been in a Princess Tower before. Never in our whole entire lives.

So we don't call out to Mum. We just keep crossing the road, until we are standing on the other side, just outside the Princess Tower.

When Mum's robot light goes green, she hurries off down the street. *'Quick-ly-quick-ly-don't-be-late,'* say her high heels. She doesn't notice we're not there.

Me and Biddy walk past the WELCOME sign, and skip up the stone steps at the entrance of the Princess Tower. Then we go through the huge wooden doors at the top of the steps.

Suddenly, we're in a ginormous archway. It is all carved with special protection beings, like shamrocks and crosses and **angels**. This tower must be a very important place to have so much magical protection.

We walk through the archway and into a massive hall. The hall has ceilings higher than the sky. It is as big as a supermarket, or a whole block of houses.

'Oh!' Biddy lifts her arms up. 'It's the Great Hall,' she whispers. 'All Princess Towers have got to have a Great Hall. It's where the balls and dances are held.'

Biddy must be right. Why else would this place be so big? See, those huge marble pillars that stretch up to infinity? Well, they must be for the ladies to lean against when they're tired from dancing. Or from waiting for the prince to fall in love with them.

The windows have coloured pictures of old kings in them, with their gold staffs and pointy king-crowns. And on the other side in the windows there are queens in veils and long dresses, just like Amira Hassan's mother—she's a Muslim lady. Each queen is holding a little prince or princess.

Today the hall is filled with seats. Perhaps the king is about to make a proclamation, and the seats are for all the people of the land to sit on while they hear him speak.

I can feel Biddy tremble with excitement.

'And when the princesses are not at a ball,' Biddy whispers, 'this Great Hall is where the people come to see the king. There's his throne and that table is for . . .' she hesitates, '. . . his stuff.'

Behind the table is an alcove filled with flowers and gold ornaments and candles. There is also a passageway that must lead into the king's private chamber.

Biddy wants to go and see the king's private chamber. I do, too.

But, then, we see a tiny, little, just-big-enough-for-one-person balcony. It is snuggled against the wall. And it's made out of a huge kind of bird statue. His claws are clutching the wall beneath him, and his wings are spread up and out behind him, to make a little railing. On the railing is a shelf. And on the shelf is the biggest book in the whole wide world.

'A **griffin**!' Biddy whispers.

'A griffin?' I ask. Of course it is a griffin. Why would they have a griffin holding a book? Griffins are the most important magical creatures in the universe. They protect sacred things.

Oo-laa-coo-laa-stinky-pooh-laa!
That book must be really special.

Biddy loves reading. I do, too. So we run towards the book. Biddy's shoes go **tink, tink, tink!** on the stone floor. And then they go **tap, tap, tap!** up the steps into the little balcony.

The balcony is so high up, we can see the whole Great Hall. But the book is even higher up than we are. Biddy stretches up on tippy-toes, trying to see the words in the book, reaching, stretching.

She can just touch the edges of the book with her fingertips. But she can't see it properly, so I go and look for her.

I run up her arm to the ends of her fingers and touch the pages. They are so soft. And they're covered in thousands and **millions** of words, all in neat rows. And running down the middle of the pages is a long silky red ribbon, like a giant bookmark.

Biddy wants to see the book for herself. She holds onto the sides of the shelf.

Then she uses her feet against the wall to pull herself up, up, **up** . . .

'I don't think that's a good idea,' a huge deep voice booms from down in the Great Hall.

Biddy spins around and ducks down behind the griffin. I run back up her arm, dive into her hair and hide.

'That is definitely not a good idea,' the huge deep voice **booms** again.

What if the person speaking is the king? What if this is his most secret sacred book that no one is allowed to look at? What if he finds me and Biddy here, and locks us in a cell high up in the tower for the whole of infinity?

Chapter seven

a dark and terrible secret

'This door must stay **locked**,' the huge deep voice says next.

Biddy sneaks up and peeks around the griffin's wing, so we can see who is talking. The owner of the huge deep voice is a **tall man** in a long dress, like a king. He and another man have just come out of a door in the side of the Great Hall. There is a sign on the door which says 'Tower Staircase'.

'No one must have access to the tower,' the king-looking person says. 'Princess Rapunzel must stay gagged and **hidden** until the time is right.'

'Yes, Your Grace,' the other man nods. He closes the door and locks it tight.

Then he hides the key on a hook behind a tapestry on the wall.

Your Grace? I think. Do they call kings 'Your Grace'? They must do.

Oh **look**! The king-looking person is holding out his hand, and there is a huge sparkling ring on it. The second man bows and kisses the ring! The king-looking person *must* really be a king. Kings often have magic rings. And people do kiss them. I've read about that. And see how the other man keeps his head bowed until the king turns away and then he walks behind.

This is too scary. Kings with magic rings are **incredibly** dangerous. If this king catches us reading his book, he will use his magic ring to turn us into toads or stars or pieces of infinity. The oldest of the terrible scoriaks from the Great Bushland can do that just by looking at you with their evil eyes. I've seen people who have been turned into pieces of infinity.

Well, I nearly have.

Anyway, I know it can happen.

Me and Biddy stay quiet as the king and the other man walk past us. They go through the alcove of gold and flowers, into the king's private chamber. The door shuts behind them, and the sound echoes briefly around the Great Hall. Then everything is silent.

'We're inside a **fairy story**,' Biddy whispers.

'Yes, Biddy! We are in a fairy story,' I yell. 'That man is a dangerous king with a magic ring. We are in a very scary situation. Let's get out of here!'

But of course Biddy can't hear me so she just ignores me.

'The king said that Princess Rapunzel must stay gagged and hidden in the tower,' Biddy whispers. 'The princess is locked in there so she doesn't run away. She has got tape around her mouth to stop her from screaming. That's what "gagged" means. And I bet she's wearing a blindfold, too. I've got to rescue her!'

'Rescue her?' I say to Biddy. 'No way! Are you mad? Do you want the king to turn us into pieces of infinity?'

What am I going to do? I've got to make Biddy understand. But she can't hear me.

What if I went right inside her ear? Perhaps I could talk straight into her thoughts. I don't want to do that, though. I don't like dark places. But I don't want to get turned into a piece of infinity either. So, it's my only chance.

Okay. I take a deep breath and dive into Biddy's ear.

Yukki-poo-la-drop-kick!

It's dark. And—**eeuu!** The walls and floor are sticky with earwax. I make myself run as fast as I can, down, down Biddy's ear canal, right to the end. There is a huge piece of skin stretched between the floor and the ceiling. It must be Biddy's eardrum.

I lean against the eardrum and whisper, as quiet as thoughts, 'Biddy. We're in big trouble. We should run away. **Quick**! Let's get out of this place now, and go and find Mum.'

I listen. I can hear the words echoing around in Biddy's brain. *'Run away . . . away . . . away. Quick . . . get out . . . out . . . out.'* And then I hear Biddy talking.

'Quick, I have to go,' she says, and I feel her stand up straight.

Yes! It worked! I run as fast as I can out of Biddy's earhole. I am so happy. But then I hear Biddy say, 'I bet Princess Rapunzel ran away from home to do **fun stuff** in the city. And the king didn't want Princess Rapunzel to have fun, so he sent his army to catch her and bring her home.'

Biddy goes on, 'And now he has locked up Princess Rapunzel in his tower.'

Biddy starts running down the stairs. 'I've got to let the princess out,' she says.

'What?' I cry. 'No, Biddy! You heard me wrong. That is not what I said. This is not play-pretend like a storybook. This is a real-life fairy tale.'

I run onto the top of her head, and tug on her fringe. 'Biddy, listen,' I say. 'We could be killed properly dead. Don't touch the door to the tower! The king will have used his magic ring to put an evil locking-spell on it.'

But Biddy just keeps running **tink, tink, tink!** across the stone floor to the door with the sign that says 'Tower Staircase'. Then she takes the key from behind the tapestry, and uses it to unlock the door.

As soon as she opens that door, we will be struck down by an evil spell.

'**Noooo!**' I cry, and burrow down inside one of Biddy's plaits. I close my eyes and wrap my arms around my head. My whole body is shaking.

Chapter eight

the monster stairwell

Click! The door to the tower staircase unlocks. **Creak!** It opens. And, **clunk!** The door closes ever so quietly behind us. I open my eyes.

We are still alive.

We are standing in a tiny room. There is a stone staircase spiralling up above our heads. It's like a cave that has been dug out from beneath the surface of the earth. Like, you know, where trolls live!

I don't like it. Not that I'm a scaredy chicken-heart lacy-petticoat or anything. It's just that stairwells are very dangerous places. All sorts of goblins and scoriaks and terrible beasties live in stairwells.

I even know why monsters live in stairwells. It's because old stairwells like this are lined with ancient humanness.

Over hundreds of years, the humans who worked in this building have climbed up these stairs to see to the prisoners at the top. And, as each human passed, they left something behind, a hair, a flake of skin, a tiny piece of toenail, a dribble of sweat.

These small pieces of humanness fall and settle in corners. They pile up, layer upon layer, along with the rat poo and cockroach feelers.

It is **true**! Look. See that grey film against the wall? The one that looks like dust? Well, that dust is really flakes of humanness. There is enough there to feed a whole tribe of terrible **beasts**.

Biddy stretches out her hands to touch the walls.

'No, Biddy!' I scream. 'Don't touch the walls. There are terrible gnashing monsters in here!'

'**Monsters?**' Biddy whispers. She pulls her hands back from the walls.

Yes! Finally she is listening to me, I think.

'Biddy, come on,' I yell, poking my head out of the end of her plait. 'Let's get out of here.'

But, she doesn't. She just tells herself firmly, using Mum's voice, 'Now, Biddy, don't be silly. There are no such things as monsters. And even if there were, you can't just run away. You've got to be brave and save Princess Rapunzel.'

'No! Biddy, please!' I scream. 'Let a grown-up save Princess Rapunzel.'

But Biddy just purses her mouth, balls her hands up into fists and starts skipping up the stairs. She sings in a determined voice, '*I am bra-ave. I am strong. I am big-ger than a, a, a, tyr-anno-sau-rus.*'

'You are **not** brave and strong,' I yell. 'You are just a little girl! And, anyway, *tyrannosaurus* doesn't rhyme with *strong*!'

But she won't listen to me, so I have to give up. I duck into Biddy's hair and hide.

The monsters are going to trip Biddy up, or bite her feet, or jump on her and **gobble** her up whole! I don't want to see it.

But, what about me? If they eat Biddy, they will eat me, too!

I've got to save Biddy, or that will be the end of both of us. I jump out of her plait. But I don't have a weapon. I must have a weapon to fight the monsters.

Then I remember Biddy is wearing a hairclip, to keep the hair above her plaits in place. Yes! The hairclip has a sharp, pointy end. I can use it for a sword.

I grab the hairclip, bend it straight to make a sword and run down one of Biddy's plaits. Then I slip into the hair elastic at the very end of the plait. With the hair elastic around my waist, I can't fall out of Biddy's hair.

As Biddy runs, her plaits swing around her head.

I **slash!** and **switch!** and **slice!** and **gash!** with my sword in the air.

My sword is ripping through the air so fast that the monsters are too scared to come out of the walls.

And Biddy never stops for a minute, so they can't grab her. Even when she gets a stitch in her side from running too much, she doesn't stop. She just breathes in deep, down into her stomach. Then she skips to change the rhythm of her running and keeps going.

She is still singing that silly song, '*I am bra-ave. I am strong . . .*'

Finally, we get to the top of the stairwell, to safety.

I raise my sword at the monsters. 'Stunned you!' I say. And, 'How's that!' And, 'Victory!'

Chapter nine

the secret room

Biddy runs into the room at the top of the stairs. 'Princess Rapunzel?' she calls. 'We have come to save you.'

But there is no one there. There's no princess tied up in the corner, with tape around her mouth to stop her from screaming. There is just a small, empty room, with a huge copper bell in the middle of it. The ringer inside the bell is tied against the bell's edge so it can't make a sound.

I skip up right on top of Biddy's head so I can see and hear everything.

'They must have hidden Princess Rapunzel in an invisible room,' Biddy says, patting the walls.

Then Biddy makes up magic words to open the secret doorways.

'Spell-in-cous-cous!' she says.

And, 'Try-la-men-ia!'

And, 'Wocca-woo!'

And, 'Stru-ta-lu-ta!'

And, 'Till-gäng-lig!'

She stops and listens after each magic word for the **creak! crack! rumble!** sounds the stone wall would make as it pulled back to reveal the secret doorway. But the only noise either of us can hear is the sound of Biddy's footsteps echoing on the wooden floorboards, and a strange hum.

What is causing the hum?

Ah! It is the great bell. The footstep-echoes are bouncing up against the wall and back onto the bell. And the sound has set the whole room vibrating with the most amazingly wonderful humming. I love it way past the furthest edge of impossibility.

'Maybe Princess Rapunzel's already escaped,' Biddy says, suddenly standing still.

'But how could Princess Rapunzel get out?' I ask, closing my eyes to help me think. How could she have possibly escaped from this tower? What happened in the story?

Oh yes! I remember.

'Biddy! **The window!**' I yell. 'She climbed out through the window.'

'Rapunzel climbed out through the window, and down her long hair!' Biddy says. Then she runs to the window so fast that I fall backwards.

And, before I can get my balance again, Biddy's head jerks forwards out through the tall slit-of-a-window.

Ahhh! I'm sliding.

Grab! Scrabble!

I catch a strand of Biddy's fringe with my hands.

But Mum has brushed it smooth. There are no knots to hang onto. The hair is slipping through my fingers. I'm falling! I'll be dead. **Splat!** Like a bug on the concrete below.

Suddenly, a rope is flying towards me. No . . . it's one of Biddy's plaits!

I grab onto it, wrapping my legs and arms around it. Then I tuck my hands and feet into its tight folds. I'm dangling high in the air, swinging through empty space. I feel a bit sick. But I'm safe.

'Holy-mog-olie!' Biddy is yelling. 'Look at that.'

I look down. The whole city is spread out below us. Everything on the ground looks tiny. Cars and people are rushing past, stopping at the traffic lights, and going on again like ants.

Right across from the tower, a lady is running backwards and forwards across the pavement. Her red coat is flapping behind her, and she is holding her high-heeled shoes in her hands.

'Mum!' Biddy yells.

And she is right. The running lady is Mum!

But Mum never runs. She always tells Biddy off for running on busy streets.

What is wrong? Something **terrible** must have happened.

There are other people running with Mum, back and forth. Police cars are pulling up at the side of the busy road with their sirens blaring. And policemen and policewomen are stopping people on the street, and asking them questions.

What do they want?

I bet Matilda wandered off on her own! She is always letting go of Mum's hand and getting lost. Matilda is such a silly, little, not-very-careful kid.

No . . . Matilda isn't lost. She's down there, too, holding a policeman's hand. Well, who are they looking for?

'**Uh-oh!**' Biddy says. 'They are looking for me!'

She leans further out the window and screams, 'Here! I'm up here. Mum! Police-people! It's okay. I'm here. **Don't worry**.'

Mum and the policemen and all the other looking-for-Biddy people are just over the road from the Princess Tower. But they can't hear Biddy yelling because she is so high up, and the traffic on the ground is so noisy.

'I'm up here!' Biddy yells again. She pulls off her shoes and waves them out of the window.

But still no one notices.

Then Biddy remembers the bell.

She pulls her head back through the window, and runs across the room to the bell. Then she undoes the rope, and swings the bell-ringer as hard as she can.

BOING! BOING! BOING! goes the bell.

It makes the loudest noise in the whole universe. My ears are ringing, nearly to bursting.

Then Biddy runs back to the window and throws her shoes out. They flutter down and bounce onto the ground, right next to a policewoman.

The policewoman looks up, sees us, waves, and calls to Mum.

Then Mum sees us, yells to the police-people, and runs straight across the road. She doesn't even look-to-the-left-to-the-right-to-the-left-again! Cars **blare** their horns and people scream. The policemen and policewomen put their hands up to stop the traffic.

And over the top of it all, Mum is **screaming**, 'Brigid Lucy!'

And, 'Stay-where-you-are!'

And, 'Get-back-from-that-window!'

And, 'Don't-you-dare-move.'

Well, we can't actually hear what she's saying, but I bet she is saying something just like that. She always does.

Chapter ten
in trouble again

Me and Biddy can hear Mum's voice yelling all the way up the stairs.

When she bursts into the bell-room, she grabs Biddy in the biggest **bear hug** ever. Then she cries and laughs and yells. She is nearly squash-suffocating me and Biddy to bits.

Then some of the police-people come in, too. The policewoman who spotted Biddy in the tower is here.

She walks over to look out of the slit-of-a-window. 'What a **view**,' she says. 'You can see the sea!'

When Mum stops crying and laughing, she wipes her face and starts telling Biddy off.

'Brigid-Lucy-what-were-you-thinking?'
she says. And, 'You-worry-me-to-death.'

Then, when Mum gets tired of telling
Biddy off, a big policeman comes over.

He kneels down, wearing a very
serious face, and tells Biddy all about
'danger' and 'strangers'. And then he tells
her how little girls should never, ever run
away from their mums because terrible
things can happen to them.

'Tell me about it!' I say. 'We just nearly
got turned into a piece of infinity by a
king's magic ring. And then we were
almost gobbled up by a huge pile of
monsters in the stairwell.'

But Biddy patiently waits till the
policeman stops talking.

Then she asks him in her most polite
voice, 'Mr Policeman, are they
allowed to keep little girls prisoners in
towers, even if they are princesses?'

'Of course not!' the policeman says.

'Well, the king is keeping a little girl
prisoner here right now,' Biddy says.

'What king?' asks the policeman.

'That one right **there**,' Biddy says, pointing at the king and the other man from the Great Hall. They have just come puffing up the stairwell.

The policeman stands up and steps towards the king.

I dive behind Biddy's ear. There is going to be a battle. The policeman will try to capture the king. The king will pull out his magic ring and cast us all into the dungeon, or feed us to a dragon.

Or perhaps he'll lock us all up here in this tower. We'll have only the terrible monsters with the gnashing teeth and sharp pointy claws for company, until the end of infinity.

But the policeman just says, 'That gentleman is not a king. He is a bishop.'

'Well, even if he is not a king,' Biddy says, 'I heard him say he was going to keep Princess Rapunzel gagged and locked up as a **prisoner** in this tower until the time was right.'

The policeman looks at the king-bishop person and asks him if what Biddy says is true.

'I'm afraid I don't know what the young lady is talking about,' the king-bishop person says. Then he looks at the huge bell. 'Ah,' he says and smiles at Biddy. 'Princess Rapunzel, you say?'

He walks over to the bell, and adds, 'You may have heard me talking about our new bell, Pristus Repastelle.'

'Pree-stuss Re-past-el?' Biddy asks, following him.

'Yes. Isn't she beautiful?' says the bishop. (Who perhaps isn't a king after all.) He points to the edge of the bell. 'See, her name is written right there.'

And he is right. *Pristus Repastelle* is engraved in delicate writing along the bell's rim.

'*Pristus Repastelle*,' Biddy reads. 'So, why did you say she had to be gagged, and that no one could see her, if she is just a bell?'

'She is not *just* a bell,' the bishop says. 'This is a **cathedral** bell. It is normal for a cathedral bell to be kept gagged, so it can't make a sound until the day it gets consecrated.'

'What does *con-se-cra-ted* mean?' asks Biddy.

'It's like a very special blessing,' says the bishop. 'And then the gag is taken off the bell, and she is rung so loudly, she can be heard all over the city.'

'Like she rang today, when I undid the rope?' Biddy asks, smiling proudly.

'Yes,' says the bishop. 'We were trying to keep her a surprise. But you let the cat out of the bag.' He looks at the policeman and the policewoman and laughs. 'Or, rather, the bell out of the tower,' he adds.

Then the bishop, the policeman, and the policewoman all look at Mum and laugh.

And Mum smiles back. Which makes me and Biddy think that perhaps Mum realises that everything that happened wasn't all Biddy's fault.

And we also think that Mum might have **forgiven us** for getting lost and found at the Princess Bell Tower.

But she hasn't.

Biddy's shoes are lost at the bottom of the tower. We can't find them anywhere.

And Mum is still so worried-half-to-death that we have to catch a taxi home instead of the train. So we don't get to see the Princess Bell Tower through the train window again.

And as soon as we get home, me and Biddy get sent to her room, to wait all afternoon by ourselves, till Dad comes home.

Then both Dad and Mum come in to talk to Biddy about running away.

Biddy tries to explain that she didn't actually run away. She tells Dad and Mum that she was just **looking** at the Princess Tower, and that she was going to come

straight back. Except there was a poor, tied-up, captured Princess Bell there, that wasn't allowed to ring.

'How would you feel if you were a bell that couldn't ring?' Biddy asks Dad and Mum.

Which makes Dad stand up and yell. Mum has to tell him to **calm down**.

This means Dad has to close his mouth tight for a moment.

Then, when he has calmed down, they both talk to Biddy for another ages, nearly forever! Until Biddy promises to never run away ever again in her whole entire life.

And then we all lived happily ever after.

Epilogue

Except that me and Biddy are grounded-for-the-rest-of-her-life. Which means we are **never, never** allowed to go and play with Jamie next door, even if we ask really nicely!

Jamie is allowed to come over to our place. But he doesn't because he still doesn't want to be a dog.

And when Mum goes to the city for another very-important-meeting, me and Biddy have to stay at home with a babysitter to look after us—even though we are totally not babies.

I usually **hate** being grounded and babysat.

But not today.

Today, Granny is babysitting us. So we are building castles in Biddy's room and deep, dark caves under her bed. And cleaning out the linen cupboard and finding exciting stuff like Biddy's old sheets from when she was a tiny baby.

And look! Granny's found a very round glass ball.

'It's a crystal ball!' Biddy says.

And it is! You know one of those kind-of crystal balls that witches and wizards use to see into the future.

We take it into Biddy's room and, the most amazing thing happens . . .

Ooops! I shouldn't have said that.

No, I can't tell you because we have run out of pages. This book is full. I will tell you that story in another book.

See ya!

Magical creatures

Nefariouses —danger rating— tremendously acutely high

Nefariouses are beautiful ancient female beings made entirely of grumpy and annoyedness. They live inside the bark of trees. They like absolute silence, so they can make up their evil poems and spells in peace. They have been known to eat noisy children. If you find yourself in a quiet place, never, ever make noise just for fun. The nefarious who made that silence will gobble you up dead.

Fillikizard dragons—danger rating—
tremendously acutely high

Fillikizard dragons are small crocodile-like creatures that have a frill of armour around their necks. They are very powerful hunters. Their back legs spin around like wheels, so they can run terribly fast. They have such huge mouths, they can eat other creatures twice their size. Never try to capture a fillikizard dragon, because they can kill you dead with a blast of their foul breaths from three metres away. If you are too big for them to swallow up, they will slobber all over you and you will stink forever.

Scoriaks—danger rating—very high

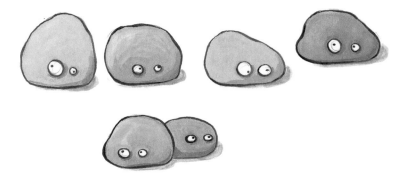

Scoriaks are big, heavy, male creatures that live inside rocks. They are so old that they came into being before the earth began. Their favourite hobbies are sleeping and thinking. If you make a noise and wake them up, they will growl and rumble, and split the earth open. Then they will swallow you whole. Or, if they are too lazy to split the earth open, they will turn you into a piece of infinity with just one look of their evil eyes. Be extremely careful when you move rocks around. Sit beside the rocks first to see if you can hear a soft snore. If you can, back away very quietly and go and find another rock to move.

Yebil yebils—danger rating—a bit high

Yebil yebils are mischievous little creatures that love to see children get hurt. They own every piece of earth in the whole wide world. They demand that everyone ask permission to walk anywhere. If you don't ask permission, they will pretend to be a piece of vine or a rock or a hole in the footpath and trip you over. Then they bend over laughing and squeal with delight. Make sure you always call out, 'Please can I play on this earth?' before you go walking in a new place.

Ympes—danger rating—low

These tiny creatures can join themselves to, and become part of, other animals and plants. They often glue themselves to a bird's feathers and fly all over the world as part of that bird. They can also melt into a tree and grow there, making the blossom on that part of the tree a different colour to the blossom on the rest of the tree. They also climb into a horse's ears and take control of the horse, so it runs around the paddock, kicking and bucking and bolting, for no reason. Always check your horse's ears for ympes before you go for a ride.

Magical swearwords

Wizz-bang-le-flab!
Oo-laa-coo-laa-stinky-pooh-laa!
Yukki-poo-la-drop-kick!
Holy-mog-olie!

Magical spell words

Spell-in-cous-cous!
Try-la-men-ia!
Wocca-woo!
Stru-ta-lu-ta!
Till-gäng-lig!

Look out for …

When Biddy's pet slug has a terrible accident, Dad buys Biddy a pet goldfish called Rolly Polly.

The invisible imp that lives in Biddy's hair thinks Rolly Polly is boring.

But then Biddy trains Rolly Polly to do tricks . . . and it's not long until things start to go wrong.

Acknowledgements

To the Tasmanian Writers' Centre, for giving me a residency in their wonderful Hobart studio where, trying to blend in with this old world and beautiful city, my little imp got me into lots of delicious trouble. To Libby and Margrete, for generously inviting me to join their table, which led to our friendship and working relationship. And, most importantly, to my niece, Brigid Tony Izod, who inspired the character Brigid Lucy.